Rockwood Hoar, William Whitney Rice

William Whitney Rice

A Biographical Sketch

Rockwood Hoar, William Whitney Rice

William Whitney Rice
A Biographical Sketch

ISBN/EAN: 9783337010836

Printed in Europe, USA, Canada, Australia, Japan

Cover: Foto ©Raphael Reischuk / pixelio.de

More available books at **www.hansebooks.com**

WILLIAM WHITNEY RICE.

A

BIOGRAPHICAL SKETCH,

BY

ROCKWOOD HOAR.

ALSO

THE WHITNEY NARRATIVE,

BEING AN ACCOUNT OF THE

WHITNEY FAMILY,

WRITTEN BY MR. RICE.

Worcester, Mass., N. S. A.

PRESS OF CHARLES HAMILTON.

311 MAIN STREET.

1897.

THIS sketch of Mr. Rice is but an outline of the life that was active, busy and useful, the source of complete happiness to those to which it was most closely allied. Possessing to an eminent degree the strong qualities and public spirit that make a man serviceable to his fellow-men, he also had the more rarely affectionate and tender nature that won the love as well as the esteem of those with whom he was associated; and it is hoped that his friends may be glad that this short record is made of one who "has done the work of a true man," and who was taken away before his usefulness was ended.

The "Whitney Narrative" was written by Mr. Rice the year after his first attack of serious illness, to divert and relieve the tedium of enforced idleness. Those to whom he read it thought it interesting, and it is now printed with the hope that it may be valued by his relatives who trace with him their descent from the Whitneys of Whitney, and by his friends as being the last completed writing of his hand.

A. M. R.

BIOGRAPHICAL SKETCH.

WILLIAM WHITNEY RICE, son of The Rev. Benjamin Rice, B. U., 1808, and Lucy Whitney Rice, daughter of Captain Phinehas Whitney, of Winchendon, was born in Deerfield, Massachusetts, March 7th, 1826, and died in Worcester, Massachusetts, March 1st, 1896.

He was seventh in descent from Edmund Rice, who came from Berkhampstead, in the County of Hertfordshire, England, and settled in Sudbury, in 1638 or 1639.

On his mother's side he was eighth in descent from John Whitney, who came from Whitney, on the banks of the Wye, and settled in Watertown, June, 1635.

Mr. Rice came on both sides from the best New England stock. No man can boast a better lineage. His ancestors were men of rugged constitutions; of simple habits and lives; used to hard work; living in an invigorating climate; cautious and deliberate; accustomed to understand and to deal with matters of general moment, so as to take an intelligent part in town meeting, on the jury, in the legislature, in town or church affairs; weighing each proposition advanced from platform or pulpit in the balances of conscience and common sense; self-reliant; respecting themselves; willing to accord respect to others. They lived in communities where there was no great contrast between poverty and wealth, unpoisoned by the discontents which envy of great fortune and great luxury often brings. They could discriminate and decide which field to plant, which task to do, which way to vote, which doctrine to believe, which thing to live contentedly without; and they knew how, "having done all, to stand."

Their opportunities were limited; their occupations often humble. How silent they were as to their own affairs, as to the stories of the men from whom they sprung! How little in detail we know about them! Yet it made small difference with the race in what places their lines fell. Its sons had the capacity to fill places of importance and to deal with great things well when the demand came. Trace the lines of descent of our great men and one will find men and women,—strong, simple, steadfast,—living, it may be, uneventful lives, but handing down sterling qualities, unalloyed, from sire to son.

From such a stock came Mr. Rice. He was proud of it. He studied his family history with loving care. In the summer of 1892 he visited the home of his maternal ancestors in Whitney, England. He aided in placing a jubilee window in the church, and at the Rector's suggestion a tablet to his memory has been placed beneath. He gained the friendship of a charming and accomplished lady,—Miss Jane Dew, daughter of the Rector,—and maintained an interesting correspondence with her with reference to the Whitneys. From information thus obtained, and from his own study and memory, he wrote a sketch of the family, which is given in this volume.

Mr. Rice's mother lived to the great age of ninety-four, dying in 1893. She was a woman of unusual force of character. He was a most devoted son. Indeed his deep attachment to his family was one of his most striking and commendable traits, directly inherited from her. He attributed much of such success as he gained to her influence. Her care and foresight made it possible that from the slender resources of a minister's household he received his academic and college education. Her pride and ambition impressed the boy with a desire to succeed.

When a little over two years old he was taken by his father in the family chaise from Winchendon to New Gloucester, the little fellow sitting on a stool at his father's feet and his mother holding the baby sister in her arms. One trunk was fastened behind, another swung from the axle; and thus the family horse, which had been purchased by its master before William's birth and survived in faithful service until after the pastor's death, drew the household for four days along the northern roads, until from a lofty hill they looked down upon the village of New Gloucester, Maine, which was to be their home for seven years. The father in his preaching in various places, while looking for a settlement, had much admired the village and pointed it out with great satisfaction to his good wife. "Give me old Massachusetts," said the tired mother. "Give me Massachusetts, too," lisped the little son. The love for his native State grew with the boy; and the days of the man were spent within her limits and in her service.

In New Gloucester, and in Buxton, not far removed, Mr. Rice's boyhood was passed, until at the age of thirteen he entered the Academy at Gorham, Maine. There he got his first systematic training. He had attended public school but little, and had learned all that he knew from his parents or by private teaching, and had developed a fondness for reading and an aptitude for reciting well. He attributed this largely to the excellent teaching of Horatio Woodman, in whose private school he learned the art of reading aloud from a master who had, besides, a discriminating taste and knew how to awaken in his scholars a love for the best literature. The boy had an excellent memory. These qualities placed him in a conspicuous place at the Academy; and he left it, at the end of three years, its best speaker and writer and its best scholar. He had a capacity for leadership among his fellows which marked his course all through his life at Bowdoin College, from which he was graduated in 1846. One of his friends, the Rev. Egbert C. Smyth, D.D., of Andover, in a tribute paid to his memory before the American Antiquarian Society, April 23rd, 1896, said:—

"I certainly do not arise with any thought of adding completeness to the tribute which is paid by Mr. Chase (in the report of the Council), but it has occurred to me while I have been sitting here that I have some remembrances of Mr. Rice which no one else may be in possession of, and think I may be pardoned for referring to them in a very few words.

"It so happened that I entered Bowdoin College when Mr. Rice was beginning his junior year. We became associated in one of the secret societies, which were then somewhat novel, and I recall with the greatest pleasure the interest which he communicated to the meetings of that association, both in a literary and social way. But I would especially recall the very prominent part which he took in college as a leader in what one may call its public life. The college was then divided into two general societies, as was still the custom of Harvard and Yale and other institutions of learning. For one, I have been sorry that in these institutions of learning those general societies have quite disappeared; no doubt there is some good reason for it, but they certainly filled a part in college life and in training men for future careers, and I do not see how this could have been better accomplished.

"There were many men who were not members of

any club or any secret society, but seldom did a student fail, as early as was practicable, to unite himself to one or the other of those general societies. They were literary in their objects. Those who were connected with them will remember with what interest what was called 'the paper' was listened to, and how wide-spread was the desire in college so to write our English language that those who had the editorship of the papers would be pleased to admit the contribution. There was a great stimulus in it. And beyond that, they were societies for discussion, and if any man in college had the capacity latent within him, it was brought out.

" Among the men who were most prominent was our late associate, Mr. William W. Rice. I suppose, indeed I am sure, there was no honor which the overseers and the faculty of the college could bestow upon the student which was prized so highly as to be elected the president or orator of one of those general societies.

" Mr. Rice, without any rival, was chosen orator, and I remember well how he fulfilled his part. There was always a dense audience when the oration and poem were delivered, and an interest was called forth in the educated community something like what is now excited by a game of football, or baseball, or a race in boats.

" Mr. Rice was a leader naturally and spontaneously. He had a capacity for public affairs, which I cannot but think, if illness had not fallen upon him, and if he had been, I may venture to say in a high and honorable sense, a little more ambitious than he really was, would have made his public life even more illustrious than is shown in the record which he has left behind."

While in college he taught school during the vacations; after graduating he began teaching in Maine, but was obliged to desist, after a month's work, because of a serious illness from which he did not recover for a year. In his senior year he had essayed successfully the feat of moving a great stone which had challenged the strength of the strongest students, and the strain of the effort had brought on a trouble in his back, so serious that he was barely able to deliver his graduating oration. He was taken from his school to his father's home in Winchendon, Mass., and there, before his own recovery, his father died.

In the fall of 1847 he had so far recovered that he resumed the occupation of teaching at Leicester Academy, where he remained for four years. The Academy was an excellent one, attended by pupils of either sex. Many persons, since risen to places of great eminence and usefulness, were his pupils. He won and retained their affectionate regard, and his days there were very happy. There he met as a pupil Miss Cornelia A. Moen, sister of Philip L. Moen, late President of the Washburn & Moen Manufacturing Company of Worcester, to whom he became engaged and whom he married in 1855, as soon as his professional income as a lawyer enabled him to establish his own household. From this union his children were born: William Whitney, Jr., who died in early childhood; and Charles Moen, H. U. 1882, who was admitted to the bar and to his father's firm and who is in active practice in Worcester. She died in 1862.

One of his pupils, at Leicester, for whom and for whose charming wife Mr. Rice always retained a most affectionate feeling, has described the academy and his teacher with much vividness. The Honorable John E. Russell says:

"Leicester Academy in 1849 was an important institution: it was the chief 'seat of learning' in the county. Its pupils, of both sexes, came from all surrounding towns. The head master, Josiah Clark, was an eminent scholar. Its annual examination and 'exhibition,' held in the 'Orthodox Meeting House,' drew crowds of people who not only filled the pews of floor and galleries, but stood at the open windows, upon wagons drawn up against the side of the building.

"It was a prosperous institution, and the co-education of young men and maidens, who boarded with the excellent families of the town, made an interesting and sparkling society.

"I was sent to Leicester under the charge of Josiah Clark, where I remained from June to November, 1849, participating in the annual exhibition of August 15th. Great and eventful day! Here I found Mr. Rice. He was very young, but had a gravity and repose of manner uncommon in youth and in our race ; to this add a large figure and a forehead already growing bald, and you have an impressive personality.

"He had a fine, clear complexion, and his hair was beautifully curly. His speech was measured and his voice sonorous. He taught English branches, and I was pounding at the classics, so I was in only one of his classes,—it was reading, much taught and practiced in those days. He loved elocution ; rejoiced in rolling rhetorical passages, in glowing poetry. The class was large and we stood and read to and at one another, largely from the speeches which Dr. Johnson wrote for the *Gentleman's Magazine*, and attributed to the statesmen of the last century.

"Mr. Rice also had charge of the 'speaking' and compositions, which came alternate Wednesdays. These exercises required rehearsals and consultations, and the weighty preparation of the Exhibition was toward, for which I was at once drafted and found myself happily in continued contact with Mr. Rice.

"I was in my sixteenth year. I think he was twenty-three. He was very affectionate in his disposition and we became exceedingly intimate. I had seen a good deal of the world, as we both thought; had been winters in New York and could tell him of the theatres and other metropolitan delights. I was in his room, which was at the academy building, of which he was in charge, every evening. We read poetry together, especially Byron and Macaulay's essays. He drilled me patiently in declamation.

"The Exhibition, largely the result of his work,

was a great success.   There was a play, founded on the Canadian Rebellion of 1837, in which Richard Olney and I were two 'Patriot' soldiers.   There was a Latin colloquy and a Greek play, and declamation galore.   Hon. Pliny Merrick gave an address, and all the eminent Esquires of Worcester, and all the Clergy were present.

"There was a row of girls in the gallery never to be forgotten.   The one you mention was certainly up to her reputation, which is not yet forgotten; and Cornelia Moen, with whom Rice was deeply in love, and whom he married as soon as he could, was a charming, dignified and accomplished girl. She looked like her father.   She was a stately figure.   She spoke French like her native tongue, and was fond of literature.

"In November, 1849, I went back to Jones' school at Bridgeport, but kept up an affectionate correspondence with Rice."

While at Leicester Mr. Rice took part in his first political campaign, and cast his first ballot, in 1848, for Martin Van Buren and for Charles Francis Adams.

He left Leicester in the year 1851 and began the study of law in the office of Emory Washburn and George F. Hoar.   After three years spent in its study he was admitted to the bar and entered almost at once into a large practice.   Worcester was then a city of fifteen thousand inhabitants.   He lived to see its population one hundred thousand.   Its people were largely engaged in a great variety of manufactures. Its mechanics were skilled workmen, receiving good pay, rising often from the shops of their employers to a business of their own. Many manufacturing towns and thriving villages brought their business to the county seat. The bar had eminent leaders. With them Mr. Rice had to contend, and among them to make a place. He took almost immediately a prominent part in the life and activities of the city. While still a law student he was elected to his first office, as member of the School Committee, serving as its Secretary for several years, and remaining upon the board until his election as Mayor. He had a business sense which made him a wise adviser of business men. He knew the motives which influenced, and the arguments which appealed to his fellows, and won a prominent place as an advocate. He became a political leader. His strong sympathies were for freedom. In 1854 he was an active member of the Worcester County Kansas League. In 1855 he records in his diary the sheltering and assisting a fugitive slave who, while on his way to Canada from Boston, saw his master and an officer enter the front of the railroad car in which he was riding, and escaping from the other door fled for protection and help to Worcester. He was an ardent supporter of Henry Wilson in his election to the office of United States Senator in that year. In 1855 he was appointed Special Justice of the Police Court. In 1858 he was appointed Judge of the Court of Insolvency, and held that office until its duties were united with those of Judge of Probate.

In the year 1860 he was elected Mayor and held that office for one year. He was the first Republican and the youngest man ever elected to that office in Worcester. During his administration, and largely through his powerful aid, the establishment of a Free Public Library, upon an adequate scale, was secured.

In 1868 he was elected District Attorney, and filled that office with great ability until his resignation in 1873.

During his professional career he was associated in partnership, first with the Honorable Thomas L. Nelson, now Judge of the U. S. District Court, later with the Honorable Francis T. Blackmer, for many years District Attorney in the Middle District of Massachusetts, and last with Henry W. King, and with his son, Charles Moen Rice, the partnership continuing until the father's death.

In 1875 he went to the Massachusetts House of Representatives, in order to lend his efficient aid to the defeating of an attempt to divide Worcester County.

September 28th, 1875, he married Alice M. Miller, daughter of Henry W. and Nancy Merrick Miller, who survives him.

In 1876 his brother-in-law, Mr. Hoar, was chosen

United States Senator at the close of his fourth term in Congress, and Mr. Rice was nominated and elected Representative from this district. He held that office for five consecutive terms. During these ten years his services were of great value to his constituents, not only upon the floor of the House and in his work upon committees, but also in responding to the numberless demands which the business and personal interests of such a constituency constantly present.

In his speech in 1880 before the Republican Convention which nominated him, he thus described his district :

"This district, as much if not more than any in the land, illustrates the effect of Republican principles. Its school-houses are open to rich and poor alike. Every ballot falls as free and unchecked as the leaves from the trees or the snow-flakes from the sky. The man who would change or coerce or conceal one of those evidences of a freeman's will, could not breathe our air or live upon our soil. Our financial institutions, safely through the depression consequent upon the war, are prosperous and attest the wisdom of the system of which they are a part. We do not want them changed. Our manufacturing interests, in all their manifold varieties, are prospering again under the influence of Republican principles. The hum of every spindle is the music of republicanism, and every steam cloud curling above our cities and villages is a spray in its wreath. Our farmers are rich and prosperous in their contiguity to the market of our cities and villages. We want no change ; we adhere to the old cause and will be found among the foremost in the grand rally about to be made for the integrity of the government and the preservation of business prosperity, for the equality of the law, and the protection of all in the enjoyment of their legal rights ; for the great principles of nationality, liberty, and union."

During all but one of his terms of service the Democratic party was in the majority in the House of Representatives and therefore the Republican members were unable to control legislation so as to carry through new measures, and only the places of the minority were open to them upon the committees. Yet Mr. Rice served on many important committees and won distinction by his ability and industry. In a review of his services in the *Boston Journal*, of September 21st, 1882, it is said:—

"Representative W. W. Rice was appointed a member of the Committee on Foreign Affairs and on Indian Affairs, as well as a member of the select committee for additional accommodations for the Congressional Library. The most important bill of a public character which he introduced was one to terminate the provisions of the treaty of 1871 with Great Britain relative to the fisheries. His list of reports shows he was a very conscientious member of that committee. His report on the Congressional Library Building will be a permanent authority on that subject, even if the scheme which he has so much at heart for the construction of a new library building should fail. His report from the Committee on Foreign Affairs on the brig *General Armstrong*, on Fisheries, on St. Johns and St. Francis River bridges, and on the Venezuela Mixed Commission leave nothing more to be said upon these subjects. They are exhaustive treatises on every one of the matters to which they relate and some of them will have a permanent value as historical works. There is no better chapter of that portion of American history to which it relates than Mr. Rice's report on the brig *General Armstrong*, and he had the satisfaction of seeing the bill upon which he had spent so much labor finally become a law after it had been before Congress for a quarter of a century. His report on the Fisheries is an exhaustive treatise, and is one from which Congressional reports will be compelled to draw their facts. From the Committee on Indian Affairs he submitted a report on the traditions of the Sioux and Dakota Indians. His principal speeches were on the following subjects: on the death of General Burnside; on the appropriation for Cherokee Indians; on Chinese Immigration ; on the Congressional Library; on the brig *General Armstrong ;* on the international fishery question; on the bill to protect innocent purchasers of patented articles; on the bill granting the right of way through the Indian Territory to the St. Louis and San Francisco Railroad Company; on the proper reference of questions relative to treaties; and on the transfer of War Department records to the State Department Building. Mr. Rice was constant in attendance upon the investigation of the Foreign Affairs Committee into the Chili-Peru business, and his work is seen in the exhaustive report of that committee, although it is not directly credited to him."

Mr. Rice was a close personal friend and an ardent admirer of Mr. Blaine, and felt most keenly the latter's defeat in 1884. Had Blaine been elected President, Mr. Rice's friends might well have looked for his advancement to some position of still greater importance and responsibility, where his capacities would have won him a wider fame.

At the close of his fifth term he was a candidate for re-election, and, after a close and exciting contest, he was nominated by the Republican Convention by a majority of one vote. The feeling aroused in the preliminary struggle was most intense. His desire for a re-nomination was not personal, but he consented to stand as a candidate upon the imperative demand of many of the leaders of his party. Unfortunately party differences among Republicans were not laid aside when the result of the convention was ascertained. The District was carried by the Democrats, and his former pupil, the Honorable John E. Russell, was elected for a single term.

This ended Mr. Rice's public career, but not his active and constant interest in public matters, and in the welfare of the community in which he lived.

He returned to Worcester and resumed the active

practice of his profession. He became again the wise adviser of our business men. He took his place on the parish committee of the Unitarian Church—the Church of the Unity—to which he was attached, and gave liberally to its support. His eulogy at the occasion of presenting to the Court the resolutions of the bar upon the death of the son of his former partner, is remembered as most affectionate and tender. He was a most public-spirited citizen. No feeling of personal regret or of personal disappointment tinged his speech or action, or withheld his ready support to any good enterprise.

He received the degree of LL.D. from his College in 1886, and served as one of its overseers. He was a member of the American Antiquarian Society, a Trustee of Leicester Academy, of the Worcester Polytechnic Institute, and of Clark University. Until his death he was the Solicitor and a Director of the City National Bank.

In 1884 he delivered the address at the centennial of Leicester Academy.

In 1892, with his wife and with Senator and Mrs. Hoar, he visited Europe, spending his time principally in England. It seems strange, wide as was his reading and deep as was his interest in English history, that he should not have gone abroad many years before; but he was a poor sailor and had a great dread of the effects of a sea voyage.

His mother had been an invalid for many years,
and his devotion to her, and his wife's devoted care
of her own parents, made them reluctant to under-
take a long absence, until his own health seemed to
require it.   The voyage and the journey were a
great delight to him, and he returned much im-
proved in health.   His vigor, however, failed, and
he was compelled to give up hard work.

He then passed each summer upon the farm in
Winchendon, which his mother had owned, and
where his brother, Charles J. Rice, formerly County
Commissioner, had lived.   It was the town where
his father had died, the home of his mother's people;
and he loved it.

His last years were exceedingly pleasant.   Sur-
rounded by a devoted family and affectionate friends,
rallying from one severe and alarming illness, he
saw his end draw near with unfaltering courage
and calmness.   Had he lived six days longer, he
would have attained his threescore years and ten.

His death was attended with many marks of public esteem: from the city, over whose destinies he
had presided in his youth, and where he had so long
dwelt, conspicuous among its distinguished citizens;
from the business institutions, and institutions of
learning, to which he had given such efficient service; from the Bar, to which he had been so long
an honor and an example; from many friends, distinguished and humble, whose grief was deep and

sincere. Perhaps no more fitting tribute to his
memory could be chosen than the estimate which
Senator Hoar gave of him to the daily press, when
the news of his death was made public. It is as
follows:

SENATOR HOAR'S ESTIMATE.

This has been a sorrowful week for Massachusetts.
Ex-Gov. Robinson, the eloquent orator, the wise
counsellor, the champion who defended the honor of
the Commonwealth in time of sorest need, has been
stricken down while still in the prime of his useful
and honored life. The sad news comes this morning, that our beloved Governor, on whose eloquent
lips his fellow-citizens have so often hung delighted,
and for whom they looked to a long career of usefulness and distinction, is stricken by the fatal
arrow. And now our own city has to mourn the
loss of her veteran servant, whose figure has been
so familiar to our streets for nearly fifty years; the
story of whose life is the story of her own life
during her growth from the thriving country village
to the great, opulent and powerful city; whom she
has honored in every variety of public service and
station,—Mayor, Representative, Judge, District
Attorney, Congressman,—he has given up his life,
full of years and honors, and the places which have
so long known him shall know him no more.

I have been asked to give my estimate of the

character of Mr. Rice. His public character, the political life which began with the foundation of the Free Soil party in 1848, and which, so far as his powerful influence went, ended only with his life itself, is familiar to our own community and will be better described by others. But I have known him with an intimate friendship from a time before his removal from Leicester, where he was a teacher, to Worcester. We were born in the same year. Although slightly my elder, he pursued his professional studies in my office, and when he completed them, in 1854, opened an office next to mine. Our places of business, with an interval of perhaps one year, have been in the same building, upon the same floor, and have adjoined each other.

I have been his associate and his antagonist in many important trials. He succeeded me as Representative of this District in Congress. We made a journey together to Europe. We were associated together for many years in the administration of the Worcester Polytechnic Institute, of Clark University and in membership of the Antiquarian Society. We belonged to the same Church. Our wives are sisters and our children have been friends. We held the same political opinions. So I think that if I ever have known any man through and through, in and out, in public and in private, I knew Mr. Rice, and I am glad to put my estimate of him upon record.

He was as absolutely perfect as any man I ever knew in the domestic relations; as a son, a father, a brother and a husband. He loved his parents, his brothers and his sisters, his wife and his children with an absolute, considerate, self-sacrificing affection, which I think left them nothing to desire, and which I think in the lot of humanity could not be surpassed. I do not think that it ever occurred to him to think of his own interests in his desire to serve them.

He was a model of the professional character. He was an eminent advocate, largely employed in important cases. He was always courteous to his antagonists, faithful to his clients and respectful to the court. He was a sound lawyer and a skilled manager of causes before juries. He was in the very first rank of the very able Bar of Worcester County, almost from the time he became a member of it until his death. Any client was safe in his hands, no matter who might be retained on the other side. There was no danger that he would lose any case that he ought to win, either before the jury or before the full bench. But in this department of professional service he had a good many competitors, some of whom undoubtedly achieved a reputation equal to his, and in a few instances a reputation superior to his. But he had, in my judgment, no equal among the members of the Worcester County Bar in one very important

department of the profession,—he was the most
sagacious adviser I have ever known of business
men who were in difficulties, or who had important
controversies which required the advice of a counsellor who knew what was best to be done in the
conduct of business, and at the same time competent
to be trusted as adviser as to their legal rights.

I have known very intimately all the great law-
yers of my time in the County of Worcester and
many of those in other parts of the Commonwealth.
It has probably been my fortune to be on intimate
relations with as many of the famous advocates of
the United States as any man now alive.　One
Attorney-General was my brother, one was my
partner, and a third was a near kinsman.　I can
only repeat what I have said many times, that in
the quality and capacity I have just mentioned, I
never knew a man that approached Mr. Rice.

He was a man of absolute professional integrity,
straightforward, direct, simple and absolutely honorable in his methods.　He was one of the assignees
of the Quinsigamond Manufacturing Company at
the time of its failure.　I was employed by the
assignees as the counsel and knew all about the
settlement with the creditors.　The business was
continued a little while by Mr. Rice, and then a settlement was made and a large percentage of the
debts paid.　I think there were complicated questions of law enough in that case alone to have

amply supported the entire Worcester Bar for three years.

He was a public-spirited citizen. He was always ready to contribute largely to all good causes. He was always ready to do his share of work in the administration of public institutions. The Polytechnic Institute owes very much to his constant and unfailing interest. He was one of the most important members of the Board of Directors of the Clark University; was a Director and Solicitor for many years of the City Bank, during a term of years covering several periods of great anxiety in that institution. He was Chairman of the Parish Committee of the Church of the Unity, and always an influential member there. He always attended the meetings of the parish until the failure of his health.

I do not think that the Worcester District has ever had a member of the National House of Representatives who was more popular with his associates. Mr. Rice spoke but seldom. I believe that he had but one speech printed in pamphlet form during his whole ten years of service, though I may be mistaken in this regard. But he understood our foreign relations, and during his term of service on that committee, was very influential in shaping the policy of the administration in regard to the fisheries. The Gloucester fishing industry looked to him as their champion and defender in the House.

He understood thoroughly the question of the tariff and the business interests of his constituents. He was a popular speaker at public meetings, especially among the people of Maine, where they have always demanded a very high order of what is called "stump oratory." His term of administration as Mayor was singularly successful and satisfactory. He would doubtless have been continued in that position had he been willing.

There is scarcely an interest or an institution in our diversified city life in which he will not be missed so long as men are living that remember him. There was never a better bank director, never a better guardian or trustee or manager of the affairs of widows or orphans, never a more faithful counsellor to men in difficulty, never a better son, father or husband. He bore the agony of a fatal sickness, lasting with brief intermissions of health, for more than three years, with an unfailing courage. During the whole of it, he thought only of the distress it would cause to his household, and never, so far as I could see, to himself.

No community is so rich in men having these qualities that it can afford to spare a man like him. There is no man left, however large his influence, however wide his fame, however brilliant his success, however great his mental capacity, however spotless his moral worth, who might not well be content, and whose children might not be well content, if, when the story of his life comes to be summed up, the scroll shall bear as honorable a record as that of WILLIAM W. RICE.

The following notice from the full heart of a close friend, who has since joined the mighty host of those who have "gone before," may well be added as a closing tribute: —

IN MEMORIAM.

In the death of Hon. W. W. Rice the whole city may well mourn the loss of one of its ablest and strongest men. Of eminent ability and strong personal convictions, he possessed a largeness of heart that embraced within it all classes of his fellowmen. To his intimate friends his death brings almost an irreparable loss. Hours spent with him in social and familiar intercourse were full of interest, and now more than ever bring up sweetest recollections. Of extended reading and rare conversational powers, there was a personal magnetism about him that drew one irresistibly towards him, and made his words soothe the irritated, inspire new courage when despondent, and always gave one a higher faith in life and its possibilities; or, quoting from one of his addresses, his words were "like pebbles dropped into the lake, which sink out of sight, but the ripples they stir touch the farthest shore." His life was full of goodness, of charities that let not the left hand know what the right hand doeth. With an almost reverential attitude towards all things good and beautiful, he seemed to attain an inexpressible tenderness which led to a rest and peace in living which was permanent, so that his joy in living was great; for with him, as Hawthorne says, "Happiness had no succession of events, because it was a part of eternity." In hours of sorrow his words were almost a benediction, and the simple honesty and beauty of his life will always be hallowed memory.

THE WHITNEY NARRATIVE.

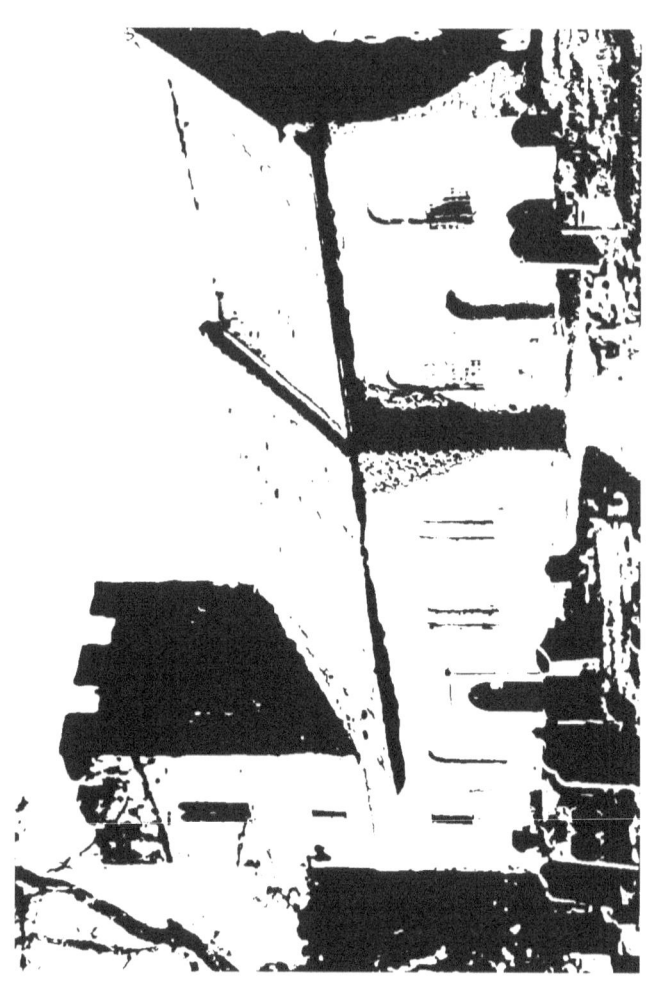

I.

VISIT TO WHITNEY-ON-THE-WYE.

It is natural for men to be interested in their antecedents. We love to search for the places of our ancestors and to trace out as much as we can of their associations and lives.

Prompted by this natural tendency, in the month of June, 1892, I took the train, accompanied by my wife, from Hereford to the parish of Whitney-on-the-Wye, seventeen miles distant, to see if perchance I could learn anything there of our ancestors.

There are none there now bearing the name of Whitney; but there are the manors of Whitney and of Clifford, formerly owned by the Whitney family, and not yet wholly alienated.

Whitney is a section of beautiful country, with an old stone church, stone cottage for the rector, and a somewhat modern manor-house, and a few other scattered houses, but no public house. We could get no public carriage for our conveyance.

We found that we had an hour and a half before the departure of the next train for London, and we resolved to make the most of that time, with such directions as we could get from the station master, who was very accommodating and intelligent. He referred us to the rector, Rev. Henry Dew, as a gentleman who would receive us hospitably, and furnish us all the information that there was to be had on the subject of our inquiries.

From the station the outlook over the surrounding country embraced in the manors of Whitney and Clifford, was as lovely as anything we had seen in England. The Wye flowed through the valley a few rods below the station, while the broad fields and forests stretched away in the distance toward the Welch mountains, which were the principal features in the landscape.

The rectory was quarter or half a mile distant. Going from the station we passed by the pretty little church. We entered the churchyard and searched for Whitney memorials. We found none, because, as we afterward learned, sometime in the middle of the eighteenth century the Wye, in a freshet, swept away the old castle, the old church, and the monuments and graves of the Whitneys from the time that they settled in that place. The new church contains many of the old granite stones which were left from the ruins of the old church. The old font, hollowed from a solid granite block, which was there before the freshet, probably from the original building of the church, and in which the Whitney infants have been baptized probably from the eleventh or twelfth century, was also recovered from the ruins and placed in the new church, where it still stands. I have a photograph of that font, taken since I was there, which I shall be happy to show to any of the modern members of the family.

Leaving the church, we went up a hill, through a lane bordered by trees, to the rectory, where we were first saluted by the vigorous barking of a black dog. A young lady, whom we afterward ascertained to be a daughter of the rector, soon made her appearance. She went to seek her father, who soon came and took us to the garden in the front of the house, where he had been working among his flowers.

He was a straight, dignified English clergyman, who, when he learned who we were and what we desired, at once gave us a cordial and hospitable welcome. He invited us into the house, where another daughter, Miss Jane, joined us. We prolonged our call there with him and his daughter as long as we could remain. Out of that call sprang a most interesting correspondence with Miss Dew, the daughter, from which I have derived much of the information made use of in the following record. I presume that I have more than twenty letters from her, generally very long and full of interesting details. I think she must have spent a great deal of her time in looking up ancient records to find material for her letters to me. I shall always entertain sincere friendship and respect for the Rev.

Henry Dew, and his accomplished daughter, Miss Jane.

Rev. Henry Dew was a brother of Sir Tompkyns Dew, the last owner of the estate. He was a descendant of the Whitneys through some one of the female members of the family, to whom the estate came by failure of the male line. Sir Tompkyns' little daughter, at the time of our visit a child about five years old, represents the broad acres of the estates of Whitney and Clifford, now, I regret to say, so heavily mortgaged that it seems quite possible, if not probable, that by the foreclosure of the mortgages they will soon pass into unknown and alien ownership. Miss Dew informs me that the payment of sixty thousand dollars would probably postpone foreclosure, and three hundred and fifty thousand dollars would suffice for the purchase of the entire estate.

I believe that the rector's tenure of the living cannot be terminated during his life; but at his death the pretty rectory, where he has lived more than fifty years and has much beautified, will pass to strangers with the rest of the estate, and thus the last Whitney traces be obliterated from the spot with which they have been so long connected.

OLD FONT,

IN

PARISH CHURCH, WHITNEY-ON-WYE.

II.

WHITNEYS OF WHITNEY-ON-THE-WYE.

Whitney, spelled in different ways, has been the name of a parish from very early days. It probably derives its name from two words signifying "white water," the first, *huit*, pronounced whete, and the second, *ey*, water, so that the word Whitney means white water, and that parish takes its name from the river Wye, which pours through it from the Welch mountains, a noisy, uncontrollable stream, the water of which is characterized by whiteness from the foam and disturbance caused by its restless passage.

Before the time of William the Conqueror the name of Whitney was borne by this tract of land; and the ancient chronicles say that during the reign of Edward the Confessor it was the property of one Alward, by his name, I should suppose, a Saxon.

Among the adventurers who flocked to the standard of William the Norman, was one of that restless race which made themselves so distinguished all over Europe in those early days as sea-rovers, coming from the North in their boats and plundering wherever they went. His name is variously written in the early chronicles as Toustain, Toustan, Tostan,

Tosti, Tostig, and Turstin. In Domesday Book it is written Torstinus, and since, in the early records, Turstin. This man seems to have been an eminent fighter among those early marauders, and there is some evidence that he was the standard-bearer of William in the great battle of Hastings. At any rate he was considered by that chief robber as worthy of great reward for his services in conquering the English; and in Domesday Book it appears that he had granted him by William some nine estates in different counties, of which the little parish of Whitney, containing about fifteen hundred acres, was one.

This parish is on the southern border of Wales, and was exposed to the incursions of those hardy descendants of the ancient Britons, who so long resisted conquest when all the rest of England had fallen. William seems to have selected some of his bravest soldiers for settlement in those frontier regions, to resist the incursions of the Welch. Here Turstin, son of Rolf, seems to have found a more peaceful life than he could have enjoyed while roaming the seas and plundering every country he could reach. Here a castle was built sometime in the latter half of the eleventh century. The ruins of this castle may still be seen on the high land in the central part of the estate.

He married a wife named Agnes Maleberge, also of Norman descent, who seems to have owned in her own right other land in the vicinity, and there at last he found a peaceful death.

He was succeeded by his son Eustacius (called *miles*, soldier or knight), who took the name of Eustacius, Lord of Whitney, and was thus, so far as I can learn, the first to bear the name of Whitney as a surname. He and his mother, Agnes, widow of Turstin, gave to the Church of St. Peter in Gloucester a hide of land (one hundred and fifty acres), for which they received due mention in the archives of the elegant cathedral in that city.

Eustacius de Whitney was succeeded by a long line of descendants, in which the names of Eustacius and Robert were the most frequent in the earlier days, after which came the more modern names of James, Thomas, John, Lords of Whitney, who were sheriffs of Herefordshire and sometimes members of Parliament, when such bodies existed. These men were royalists, as in duty bound, and became widely connected by intermarriage with other families in the vicinity and even at a distance. Of course the landed property of the family, in the process of time, became somewhat broken up, although that of the old grant, the castle and the surrounding land, seems to have remained undivided in the family, by a rule of descent not fully understood by me, and brought down perhaps to the present time.

In the earlier days the Lords of Whitney fought

against the Welch at home or followed the king
when summoned by him to foreign wars. In the
latter class of service we find the tradition of the
Lord of Whitney, Sir Randolph de Whitney, accompanying Richard Cœur de Lion to Palestine, where
he seems to have derived the crest of the family
which has remained in use to the present time.
This crest shows the head of a bull, and the following legend is found explanatory of it, which may be
received by those who please to believe it as real
rather than apochryphal:

" Sir Randolph de Whitney, grandson of Eustacius the founder of the name, son of old Torstinus,
accompanied Richard Cœur de Lion to the wars of
the Crusades, and was greatly distinguished by his
personal strength and courage. On one occasion,
being sent by Richard on a mission, the brother of
Saladin, with two Saracens in his company, followed
him, and going around a small hill, suddenly made a
vigorous attack on the English knight. De Whitney defended himself with the greatest valor, but
his assailants were gaining upon him when a furious
bull, feeding near the scene of the conflict, was
attracted by the red dress of the Saracens and
made so fierce an attack upon them that the two of
the lesser rank were driven from their intended
prey and sought safety in flight. Sir Randolph
soon succeeded in wounding his remaining assail-
ant, whom he left for dead, and then overtaking the
two other Saracens, despatched them and proceeded
on his mission. Sir Randolph attributed his escape

to the especial interposition of the Virgin. On his return to England he erected a chapel to the Virgin, the walls of which remain to this day, adjoining the grounds of the ancient family mansion, and he adopted the bull's head in his family crest at the head of a cross, beneath which was written the family motto, *Magnanimiter crucem sustine.*"

However much truth or fiction there may be in the above tradition, certain it is that the Whitneys continued to live on the estate of their ancestor Torstinus for many hundred years. Whitney castle was one in a line of fortifications built under the order of the early kings for protection against the unconquerable Welch. There the Whitneys lived and fought, married and greatly multiplied, through all the centuries, always loyal to the King and the Church. More than one of them lost their lives in the discharge of their duty.

In the reign of Henry IV., I find that the king granted to Sir Robert, Lord of Whitney, the adjoining manor and castle of Clifford.

TRANSLATION OF PATENT ROLL 5. HENRY IV. 1st Part, No. 372, Membrane 2.

" THE KING to all whom &c. greeting— Know ye that since the father of Robert Whiteney, Esquire, and his uncle and a great part of his relations have been killed in our service at the capture of Edmund Mortemer, and his property has been burned and destroyed by our rebels of Wales so

that the said Robert has not any castle or fortress where he can tarry to resist and punish our
aforesaid rebels as we have learned We, of our
special grace, have granted to the said Robert the
Castle of Clifford and the lordships of Clifford and
Glasbury together with all the lands, tenements,
rents, services, fees, advowsons, royalties, liberties,
franchises, jurisdictions, escheats, fines, redemp-
tions and other commodities whatsoever to the said
castle and lordships in any manner belonging and
also full punishment and execution of all rebels who
are or shall be of or in the above said lordships with
all forfeitures and escheats of such rebels, which
castle and lordships before that they were devas-
tated and destroyed by our aforesaid rebels stood of
the value of one hundred marks per annum as is
said. To have to the said Robert the Castles and
lordships aforesaid with all the said profits, commodities and appurtenances from the fifteenth day
of October last past, until the full age of Edmund,
son and heir of the Earl of March, last deceased
and so on from heir to heir until any one of the
heirs aforesaid may arrive at his full age. Without
rendering anything therefor to us or to our heirs at
our exchequer during the minority of the heirs
aforesaid. So always that the said Robert has
repaired the aforesaid castle and tarried in the same
in the defence and keeping safe of the castle and
lordships aforesaid. And in case that the Castle
and lordships exceed the value of the aforesaid
hundred marks per annum the said Robert shall
answer to us yearly at our Exchequer of the sur-
plusage of them as is just. In testimony whereof,

&c.—Witness the King at Westminster the 14th day of Feby. 1404.

"By the King himself."

The two estates from the date of the above, to-wit:—1404, to the present time have been united, and belonged to the Whitneys.

From the recitals in the above grant, it would appear that the service of the Whitneys in return for the royal favors was no sinecure. I do not know how many of them gave their lives in the fierce wars against the Welch, which lasted during several reigns, but it would seem that they fully vindicated the fighting character of the hardy Northman from whom they sprang.

The fair Rosamund (Rosa Mundi, Rose of the World), celebrated in history and by Tennyson in his Tragedy of Becket, in which Miss Ellen Terry represents the fair but frail country beauty, was born in the castle of Clifford before it was granted to Whitney.

Notwithstanding the grant of Clifford to Whitney on account of the destruction of his own castle, tradition soon finds him back in a new castle erected on the Whitney estate, where subsequently, on the occasion of the marriage of the then incumbent, Sir Robert Whitney, to Alice Vaughan was produced the following wedding song or Epithalamium, written by a Welch bard, which has been preserved to the present time, and a copy of which, translated

from the original Welch, has been furnished me by
Miss Dew.

EPITHALAMIUM.

Is there one on the banks of the Wye has the humour
Of Squire Robert Whitney? whom God ever bless:
Of the Cross figured mansion how staunch is the eagle:
From Trysol he takes his descent and not less.

His bridal descent, not a thought it needs further,
Thomas Roger's own daughter is her pedigree:
Tis enough if he chose Mistress Alice to marry;
Of a Sun among stars his selection will be.

Of the Court every courser with stars is bespangled;
The liquor and viands there a harbour would fill:
Past the strong towers of Robert when e'er I've to travel
His watch and his ward make my blood to run chill.

This master of mine in the towers of his father
Newgate holds not the money about him in coin:
The parish can't number his men in plate-armour,
And his steeds and his spear men the battle to join.

There sits Mistress Alice all retired in her bower,
With her money and treasures so grandly array'd;
On a Monday she puts on a fine robe of damask
Of Camlet like velvet, with pattern display'd.

O'er her cheek and her temple, of gold her attire is;
She wears garlands and scarlet in dignity great:
For the salmon's own lifetime she'll call upon Jesus,
For nine lives of a man shall she bear her estate.

All Elvael's invited, so lavish is Robert;
Of his store freely gives he to me; nor afraid
As a justice is he to deliver just sentence
When sitting in justice on some Master Cade.

There breathes not a man who shall prove him in treason
While there lives boat or ship with an anchor at sea :
Permit it he will not, he'll never give reason —
While the moon night illumine, or blue the sky be.

As all the world knows, in my Lord's lordly mansion
Are huntsmen and yeomen, that none will deny ;
In its stalls stand the coursers all gilded and neighing,
Bows for battle, and horns, and the stag's bleating cry.

In Whitney are greyhounds, of hounds too a hundred ;
There huntsmen in plenty all ready to start ;
With kitchens for Christmas, and buttery and cellars ;
While men prattle at work, many cooks ply their art.

From the mansion is carried loud laughter of peasants,
From the tower that of many an unbidden guest ;
From the bridegroom bring progeny, offspring, descendants ;
From the bride bring a blossom — a line to be blest.

Amen — I say, too, may her children content her,
And gladden the bosom of Whitney's brave Lord ;
May they grow in their mansion in lieu of good liquor,
And in the White Tower where riches are stored.

My lady's fine mansion, my lord's goodly mansion
Is the Wretches' asylum, so holy is she ;
Tower fairer than was the White Tower of London,
Is Whitney's, so bounteous and gentle is he. —

What mansion save that on the headland of Alice
Like Sandwich is fashioned like five on the dice ?
More lofty than Joseph's or Sisera's palace,
The fortress on Wye will grow ever in size.

Not dearer to me are the Houses of Charity,
By Lazarus built nor Nudd's own on the Strand,
Than Whitney's, as peerless for wine and hilarity
As flowers from the South are to ev'ry far land.

From one and the other more lavish the gifts are
Than the flow of the stream to the guileless and meek :
So the wise men gave Mary the gold from their coffers ;
From far when they travelled their Saviour to seek.

Of their gold ore and mead, goods of both and of either ;
I shall ne'er be denied by this well-wedded pair :
Their land, too, will revenue bring me, and raiment,
Divers herbs, and of feasts, too, ne'er fail me a share :

Divers dainties shall reach us from plain and from mountain,
Divers birds, too, and fishes fresh out of the sea :
He is Arthur himself so he will not o'er look me ;
His Queen, too, Gwenhwyvai, like minded is she.

Woe, Woe, to the Saxon who loves not their Castle,
Of the Welshman who scorns them be told a sad tale ;
Nor Daniel, nor Denis, Cedwyn, them to cherish,
David, Dwynwen, Elias, nor Hilary fail.

May thou live the long life both of Noee and Moses :
Of two trees, the oak female and male be their age :
Late let them be parted when death their course closes :
Mary, speedwell its outset, make happy its stage :

Yes, late be their parting : the length of their lifetime,
From Whitney to Monmouth the oldest defy ;
To bestow, with their links of pure gold many collars,
And with wine crown the bowl on the banks of the Wye.

They became connected by marriage with the
best families of the section, as witness the marriage
of Sir Robert with the fair Alice Vaughan, at whose
wedding the above bridal song was produced, the
Vaughans being among the most distinguished of
the noble families of Wales, from whom have

sprung many eminent men both in England and this country.

It is curious to notice how many descendants spring from the old family stocks. As in this country there are thousands of Whitneys from the emigrant John, so in England there have been many families, some of them at a distance from the old home, but all of them coming from the original stock of Turstin. It is not part of my purpose to follow any of these to the places where they are settled, and some of them have obtained wealth and distinction. I shall confine myself to the old stock at the old castle down to the seventeenth century.

During that time, in addition to the destruction of the castle by the Welch rebels, already referred to, there was another and more complete destruction by the freshet of the river Wye which swept away the old castle, and the old church with the graves and monuments of the Whitneys who had been buried there, and cut a new channel for itself, changing the banks of the stream so that the new church, manor house and other buildings are on the bank opposite where they originally stood. Some of the stones of the old church were built into the new church, where they may still be seen. When the waters of the river are low, immense piles of the ancient ruins can be seen, where they have been undisturbed for more than two hundred years.

4

This destruction by the freshet of the Wye occurred sometime during the first half of the eighteenth century, at which time William Warder, partly by descent and partly by purchase, seems to have been the owner of the entire estate. He was descended from a Sir Robert Whitney, all of whose sons died without issue, by a daughter Ann or Hannah, who married Robert Rodd, heir of an adjoining estate. He rebuilt the buildings which are now there, and his descendants continued to occupy them until the present time; Sir Tompkyns Dew being the last male representative, who was the father of the little girl in whose name the estate now stands. Rev. Henry Dew, the present rector, father of my correspondent, Miss Jane, is a younger brother of Sir Tompkyns, from whom he derived the living of Whitney.

The civil wars between King and Parliament, between the Church and the Puritans, were troublous times to the Whitneys of Whitney, staunch royalists and churchmen as they were. While the lineal representative of the family seems to have still lingered at the old home, yet other branches seem to have been scattered in all directions. In this dispersion we may leave the Whitneys and the families descended from them in England, and transfer our investigations to this country, which, as we shall see, has become the home, for the last two hundred and fifty years, of those with whom we have more immediate connection.

[The following notes were received from Miss Dew, after the foregoing was written.]

Thomas, father of John Whitney the emigrant, was the son of the last but one Sir Robert of Whitney.

All traces of Whitney Castle have long ago disappeared. It is marked as a ruin on Isaac Taylor's map of Herefordshire (1794), and its site was almost identical with that of old Whitney Court, which stood only a little distance from the present Court, lower down the stream (of the Wye), and of which a massive square-cut beam imbedded in the right bank and visible at low water, marks the site.

There is no trace or local tradition of the site of a chapel near the Court.

Turstin or Torstinus, *i. e.*, Turstin Fitz Rolf, left no issue. The father of Eustace de Whitney and husband of Agnes de Maleberge was therefore another Turstin. [Mrs. Dawson.]

III.

WHITNEYS IN MASSACHUSETTS.

1. July 20, 1592, John Whitney was baptized at
St. Margaret's Church, London. He was, as nearly
as I can determine, son of Thomas who was residing
at Lambeth Marsh, London, whose wife was Mary
Bray, daughter of John Bray, of Westminster.
There is evidence that Thomas was grandson or
great-grandson of Sir Robert Whitney, the last of
the name at the old castle. This branch had drifted
away into the great whirlpool of London life; and
it appears probable that it had no part or parcel
in the ancient inheritance, and had even forsaken
the faith which for so many centuries had there
been entertained, which Miss Dew maintains may
well be inferred from the Bible names the emigrant
gave his children.

The young John married Elinor, whose surname
I do not know, and lived at or near Lambeth
Marsh, at a place called Isleworth, where their
oldest children were born. In 1635, in all proba-
bility a thoroughly constructed Puritan, he, with his
wife and five children, embarked for America.
They settled in Watertown, where he continued to
reside during the remainder of his life. He seems

to have been a man of respectable character and more than ordinary education, as very soon after his arrival he was made selectman and town clerk. He also exhibited a trait of character which has been possessed by many of his descendants,—of obtaining possession of landed estates. He seems to have considered it a duty, however many children he had, to obtain a tract of land for each of them. His own homestead, where he lived after coming to America, seems to have been favorably located and in the vicinity of the best settlers of the place. He died June 1, 1673, over eighty years of age.

2. His oldest son, John, born in England in 1624, married Ruth Reynolds, of Boston, and lived in Watertown, where he died in 1692.

3. His son Nathaniel was born in Watertown, February 1, 1646, and died in Weston, January 7, 1732. According to this he would be the first Whitney to reside in Weston, which was a farming section of Watertown, ultimately set off into the new town of Weston. The cellar and well of the original Whitney house, built, as we presume, by Nathaniel, are still plainly to be seen, while a few rods distant is a more recent house in which the Whitneys resided generation after generation down to within twenty years of the present time, and which from time to time was enlarged to accommodate Whitneys, seniors and juniors.

Nathaniel Whitney married Sarah Hagar. He

died in Weston, aged about ninety. Eli Whitney, inventor of the cotton gin, was a descendant of Nathaniel.

4. His third son, William, was born in Weston, May 6, 1683. He married Martha Pierce.

5. Their oldest son was William, born in Weston in 1706. He married Hannah Harrington in 1735.

6. Their oldest son was William, born April 10, 1736. June 4, 1762, he married Mary Mansfield, and a few years later, with sons William and Phinehas, they moved to Winchendon.

Hereafter I confine myself to William Whitney and his descendants. In this connection, however, it is proper to say that Henry Whitney, probably a cousin of John, is found in Connecticut in 1649; a descendant of his, S. Whitney Phoenix, a wealthy and liberal citizen of New York, has published a genealogical account of the descendants of Henry, contained in three volumes, making one of the most sumptuous family records in America. This does not include any of the descendants of John, most of Henry's descendants being south of Massachusetts.

IV.

WILLIAM WHITNEY OF WINCHENDON.

William Whitney was born in Weston, April 10, 1736. He was married in Weston to Mary Mansfield, June 14, 1762. They had seven children. (1) William, born in 1765, married to Ann Heywood in January, 1791. He lived in Gardner, where he died in 1846. (2) Phinehas, born in Weston, April 1, 1766, died May 10, 1831. He lived in Winchendon. (3) Mary, born April 10, 1773, married to Benjamin Heywood, of Gardner, where she lived during her life. She was mother of Levi and Seth Heywood, who built up the large business in Gardner, to which that town owes so much its growth and prosperity. (4) Joseph, born May 20, 1775. He lived in Winchendon. (5) Amasa, born June 16, 1777, died February 2, 1852. He lived in Winchendon, where he was largely engaged in business. (6) Sally, born September 3, 1779, married to Smyrna Bancroft, of Gardner, where she lived. (7) Luke. He lived in Gardner.

William Whitney, Sr., seems to have begun to buy land in Winchendon as early as 1769. In 1774 we find him there taking part in the affairs of the town. He had a large farm, situated on the line between Gardner and Winchendon. He seems to have been an excellent farmer and a man of thrift, who accumulated, for those days, a handsome property. He had the reputation of being the best judge of cattle and horses in those parts. He represented the town in the General Court during several of the last years of his life. He was a man of rather more than the medium size, of sturdy and healthy frame. From descriptions given me by my mother and aunts, I think his son Amasa resembled him physically. He died in 1816.

His wife, Mary Mansfield, was a good housewife, I have been told, of very industrious and pleasant character. As they lived four miles from the meeting-house, they were accustomed to ride up to meeting on horseback, she on the pillion behind, according to the fashion of those days. She died a few years before her husband. They are buried side by side in the Whitney corner of the burying-ground in Winchendon.

William Whitney, Sr., died possessed of a farm containing six hundred and forty-eight acres, which was sold to his oldest son, William, of Gardner, for seven thousand dollars. I believe that the land of this farm, almost all of it, is still owned by descendants of William Whitney. He was an excellent farmer, a very conservative man, and a good judge of farming land and all things pertaining thereto. It is said that a short time before his death he gave to his sons, who were gathered about him, the advice, "Buy land, boys, buy land," which some of them have done not wholly to their advantage.

He was always loyal to the government and institutions of his country, like his English ancestors before him. I quote the story, handed down by tradition, as illustrative of this law-abiding character.

"At the breaking out of the Shays Rebellion, Winchendon was nearly equally divided between the government and the followers of Shays. The Governor called upon the towns to furnish recruits to put down the rebellion, Winchendon with the rest. The citizens were assembled upon the common for the purpose of obtaining the recruits to fill the quota of Winchendon. Party feeling ran high. The opponents of the government remonstrated bitterly against the furnishing of any recruits from Winchendon. As was the fashion in those days, the drummer paraded up and down, beating his drum, that those who were willing to join the company should follow him. No one did so. Old William Whitney, then, perhaps, the leading farmer in the town, was on the ground, favoring the government. Seeing that no volunteers offered themselves, he called upon his son Phinehas, then a stalwart and hardy young man, saying to him in tones that were heard by all, 'Fall in, Phin., fall in.' Phin. fell in and the company was soon filled."

I have often heard, when a child, the story of that fearful march in pursuit of the rebels, whom they overtook and scattered at Petersham. That was the first, but by no means the last, military service of Phinehas Whitney, who after that became Captain of a Cavalry Company of Winchendon and the adjoining towns, which office he held for a long term of years.

William Whitney's estate was appraised September 2, 1817, at sixteen thousand, four hundred and forty-eight dollars and twenty-seven cents ($16,-448.27); a pretty fair amount to be accumulated by one beginning in a wilderness, before unbroken, in 1774.

PHINEHAS WHITNEY.

7. Phinehas Whitney was the second son of William, Sr., and was born April 1, 1766, before his removal from Weston. He married in Winchendon for his first wife, Phœbe Stearns, January 17, 1793. She died the next year, April 7, 1794, leaving a son Phinehas, who died in early childhood.

For his second wife he married Bethiah Barrett, of Westford, February 16, 1796.

Capt. Phinehas Whitney was a very active and successful business man. He owned the tavern in the centre of the town, where he also owned and kept the country store. He also owned and carried on several farms; the largest, perhaps, that connected with the tavern.

Benjamin Wilder and Phinehas Whitney bought this tavern property,—upon which was built one of the earliest houses in Winchendon, and always used as a tavern,—and the tract of land connected with it, estimated to contain one hundred and eighty acres, for six thousand dollars, September 8, 1801, of James McElwain (pronounced "Muchelwain"). The next year Phinehas Whitney bought of Benjamin Wilder his interest in the premises, and then took up his residence upon it, and continued the tavern, which had been kept there already by several previous owners. He moved to this place from the farm known as the "Benjamin Farm," which he continued to own during his life.

He was a man of great energy and enterprise. He was accustomed to make frequent journeys to Boston for the purpose of exchanging Winchendon products for city supplies. He used to make his journeys largely in the night-time; going in the night, transacting his business in Boston the next day, and starting for home on the coming night.

He was a man of great physical strength and was active in all athletic sports, of which I used to hear stories in my childhood. He was a man fully six feet in height, with broad and sinewy shoulders and very long arms. He had brown hair—rather thin upon the crown. He was a very kind neighbor, and was one of the first to visit whoever was sick or in distress.

He always had several men in his employ who were known as capable and efficient men to work. My opinion is, that in those days, when the employer was accustomed to lead the employees in their respective departments of labor, he undertook more enterprises than he could profitably execute. Hay which was cut down in large quantities by a sturdy gang in the morning, was not always cared for and gathered before the storm; and the sheep on the distant pastures were not always safely and comfortably housed against the weather.

I remember him as a most affectionate, loving and lovable man, always attentive to the comforts of his children and grandchildren. His large family were terribly afflicted by his comparatively early death, away from home on one of his Boston trips, broken down by excessive labor. He died in Newton, May 10, 1831.

Bethiah Barrett Whitney, his second wife, was a model woman. If her husband was a tireless man of business in the outside affairs, she was as industrious and careful in all matters pertaining to the interior arrangements necessary to his affairs. She was of good Lexington stock, her mother being Anna Fiske, and her grandmother, for whom she was named, Bethiah Muzzy. Her father was Oliver Barrett, who responded as a minute-man on the nineteenth of April, 1776, at Lexington, afterwards served at Bunker Hill, and on the second day of January, 1777, enlisted in the Revolutionary Army as a volunteer from the town of Westford, and served in the Massachusetts Regiment commanded by Col. Thomas Marshall, until October 7, 1777, when he was killed in battle at the second battle of Stillwater, between the North American Army, under Gen. Gates, and the British forces, under Gen. Burgoyne. His name, by the side of his wife, is on the Whitney monument in the Whitney burying-ground, although his body is buried in an unknown grave somewhere near where he fell, at Albany, I think.

She was small in stature, with blue eyes and brown hair, leaving the impression upon the children who knew her and still remember her, of great dignity and gravity. I do not remember that she ever smiled, nor do I remember that a cross or impatient word ever escaped her lips. Through the large and complicated household affairs which she was called to superintend, she always moved with the most absolute efficiency and self-possession. I do not think that much time was wasted by the employees in her house, either at the tavern, or at the large and better house which her husband ultimately built on the opposite side of the road.

She went to Winchendon for the purpose of teaching school, for which she was well fitted; and after her marriage to Capt. Whitney she assumed the leading place among the women of the town, which she held during her life. She died at the house of her youngest daughter, Mrs. Louisa W. Lyman, in Marlborough, New Hampshire, August 2, 1849, aged 74 years and 7 months.

Her own mother, whom she is said to have very much resembled, passed the last year of her life with her in Winchendon; and they all are buried in the same corner of the old Winchendon burying-ground.

Capt. Phinehas and Bethiah Whitney had eight children, three sons and five daughters.

Phœbe Whitney, born April 5, 1797. She was a tall woman; in fact, all of the daughters inherited the stature of their father rather than of their mother. In early life it was said that she was of a very gay and social character, which could scarcely be believed by those of us who knew her only in old age as one of the gravest and most dignified of women.

She married Asa Washburn in 1817. He died in 1824. They had two sons, Nelson Phinehas Washburn, born October 14, 1818, and William Barrett Washburn, born January 31, 1820.

Nelson Phinehas Washburn married Elizabeth A. Hills, of Peterborough, N. H., February 10, 1845. They now reside at Claremont, where he is engaged in the manufacture of boots and shoes. They have had two children. (1) Helen Elizabeth, born January 3, 1847, and married to Frank P. Maynard, February 10, 1876. (2) Charles Nelson Washburn, born May 10, 1854, married to Kate Alice Brooks, September 10, 1884. Neither of these have had any children. Both Frank P. Maynard and Charles Nelson Washburn are engaged in the manufacture of boots and shoes, with their father, at Claremont, under the name of Maynard and Washburn.

Hon. William Barrett Washburn, the younger son of Asa and Phœbe, entered Yale College in 1840 and was graduated from that institution in 1844. He went into the office of his uncle, William Barrett Whitney, of whom he was the namesake, at Orange, Massachusetts, and ultimately abandoned the idea of studying for a profession, and remained in his uncle's employ until his failure in business. He succeeded to the management and ownership of the business of his uncle and soon removed to Greenfield, which was a more convenient location for carrying on the very successful business in which he was engaged, to wit, the manufacture of lumber and wooden ware.

He was a member of the State Senate of Massachusetts in 1850; of the House of Representatives in 1854; he was a member of the thirty-eighth, thirty-ninth, fortieth, forty-first and forty-second Congresses. He then was selected by the opposition to General Butler in the Republican Party for the nomination of Governor in 1871. After a canvass almost unprecedented in the history of Massachusetts politics, he was nominated in Worcester in a convention which began about eleven o'clock A. M. and lasted until past midnight. None who were members of that convention will ever forget it. Although Mr. Washburn's managers had a majority in the convention, General Butler fought with his wonderful skill and pertinacity at every step, and only yielded the victory when the result could be postponed no longer. Mr. Washburn was elected by a large majority and continued to occupy the Governorship until April, 1874, when he resigned, having been elected United States Senator to fill the unexpired term of Charles Sumner. Upon the expiration of this term he retired from public life, which he did not re-enter.

In 1872, Harvard University conferred upon him the honorary degree of LL.D. He was president of the National Bank of Greenfield until his death. He was a trustee of Yale College from 1869 to 1881. He was a member of the Board of Overseers of Amherst College and trustee of the Agricultural College, at Amherst; also of Smith College, at Northampton, and the Moody School, at Northfield. He was a director of the Connecticut River Railroad. He was a man of admirable executive and business ability, and discharged the duties of all the positions which he was called upon to fill to the acceptance of those whom he represented. In Congress he was the chairman of the committee on claims, and it used to be said of him that when he had examined a claim and decided upon it there was no need of any further examination of that claim. He was a leading member of the Congregational denomination, and died at Springfield, October 5, 1887, instantly, just as he ascended the platform of the American Board of Commissioners for Foreign Missions then assembled there.

Gov. Washburn was a man of rare ability in

everything that he undertook. His father died when he was a child; and for some years he and his brother Nelson lived with their grandfather, Capt. Phinehas Whitney, in Winchendon. Here they were expected to work, at least so they thought, beyond the strength and capacity of boys so young. He often sent them to drive droves of cattle from Winchendon to Brighton, stopping over night at the regular places, where the cattle were turned into a pasture and the boys slept in the barns or on the ground, as they might prefer. Often, too, the grandfather drove his loaded wagon from Winchendon to Boston, one of the boys following with a second wagon, often asleep on the top of the load. Sometimes one of the little fellows was sent to Boston alone, with a roll of money sewed up in his inside clothing, to do errands for his grandfather. Gov. Washburn, after this training, took a high rank in Yale College; and it is no wonder that he became an able and eminent man. He accumulated a large property; and his widow and daughters still reside in Greenfield in the old mansion-house, which he built.

Like his grandfather and great-grandfather, he had an almost instinctive knowledge of cattle and horses, which they all seem to have inherited from the old Hereford County in England, where the family originated.

He married Hannah A. Sweetser of Athol, Sept.

6, 1847. Her father was a large farmer and cattle dealer, in which business Mr. Washburn had become an adept while with his grandfather in Winchendon. They had six children, two sons and four daughters.

(1.) Maria Augusta Washburn, born November, 1849. She died in infancy.

(2.) William Nelson Washburn, born July 30, 1851. He graduated at Yale in 1874. July 21, 1880, he married Jennie E. Daniels, of Chicago. They have had two children, but one of whom survives, Lelia Atkinson Washburn, born April 28, 1884.

(3.) George Sweetser Washburn, born October 16, 1854. He died in May, 1870. He was a brilliant young man, and had begun a course of study intending to graduate at Yale, and then enter upon a professional life.

(4.) Anna Richards Washburn, born August 16, 1856. She married Walter Osgood Whitcomb. They reside in New Haven, where he is a member of the firm of Charles B. Rogers & Co., manufacturers of bedding and brass and iron bedsteads. They have had no children.

(5.) Clara Spencer Washburn, born March 18, 1860.

(6.) Mary Nightingale Washburn, born July 2, 1861.

Phœbe Whitney married for her second husband

Mr. John Woodbury, of Winchendon, in May, 1827. He died in Winchendon, December 5, 1870, aged eighty-six years and four months. They had one child, Mary Jane Woodbury, born March 11, 1828, and died October 11, 1840.

Thus Phœbe Whitney, mother of Nelson Phinehas and William Barrett Whitney, has at the present time but one grandchild of the second generation. She died at the home of her son, Nelson Phinehas Washburn, in Nashua, March 7, 1876, aged nearly seventy-nine years.

Lucy Whitney, the second daughter of Capt. Phinehas and Bethiah Whitney, born June 4, 1799, died July 18, 1893, aged ninety-four years, one month and fourteen days. She married, March 29, 1825, Rev. Benjamin Rice, of Deerfield, Mass. He died in Winchendon, July 12, 1847.

Rev. Benjamin Rice was born in Sturbridge, Mass., May 9, 1784. He graduated at Brown University in 1808, studied divinity at Andover, and graduated at that seminary in the class of 1811. He was a good man, an acceptable preacher; and his children have always remembered him as a most affectionate and indulgent father, taken from them at too early an age.

Lucy Whitney, his wife, like all the daughters of Capt. Phinehas and Bethiah Barrett Whitney, was tall in stature, of great mental and physical strength; accompanying her husband through his pastorates

in Maine and Massachusetts, she left everywhere a
most enviable reputation. When young her health
was quite delicate, and her father and mother
despaired of her reaching years of maturity. She
was, however, given for those days an uncommonly
good education for a girl. I have heard her name
some of the academies where she attended,—among
which were Bradford, Amherst and Leicester,—of
all of which I was accustomed to hear entertaining
reminiscences during my childhood. She was generally carried to and from the academies by her
father, for whom she always entertained an affection
amounting almost to idolatry. His death, in 1831,
was followed by an illness of hers, which for some
time threatened to prove fatal.

She was inspired with an impression that her
children should all be educated as she had been;
and to accomplish that end no sacrifice or labor on
her part was too great or exacting. She was
economical and thrifty in all her household affairs
that she might save money for this purpose.

After the death of her husband, in 1847, she
bought a portion of the estate of her brother, William Barrett Whitney, on which the old hotel originally stood, but which had been removed and a small
house built on the old site by her brother, and occupied by him until his removal to Orange. This
estate she occupied for many years and continued
to own it at her death.

Of course a son may be pardoned his partiality for his mother; but I can truthfully say that I never knew a woman of such determined and unconquerable spirit, of such keen perceptions and affectionate devotion as was hers. Spared through a life of unusual length, with remarkable health in her old age excepting rheumatic attacks, with an unclouded mind, taking an interest in everything pertaining to the country and her own family almost to the day of her death, she died in Hubbardston at the residence of her daughter, Mrs. Hitchcock, of no special disease but old age.

We buried her in the old burying-ground at Winchendon, where she rests by the side of her husband, and near her father and mother and grandfather and grandmother and other relatives, beneath the shadow of old Monadnock, which looked into the cradle in which she was rocked as a child.

They had three children: William Whitney Rice, born in Deerfield, March 7, 1826; Lucy Ann Rice, born in Deerfield, September 26, 1827; Charles Jenkins Rice, born in New Gloucester, Maine, July 2, 1832.

William Whitney Rice fitted for college at Gorham Academy, Maine; graduated at Bowdoin in 1846. He was sick at his mother's home in Winchendon for a year after graduation. He was a preceptor at Leicester Academy for four years. He then studied law with Hon. Emory Washburn, and was admitted to the bar in 1854. In 1858 he was appointed Judge of Insolvency, by Gov. Banks. In 1860 he was elected Mayor of Worcester. He was District Attorney for the Worcester District five years, from 1869 to 1874, but he resigned to accept an election to the Massachusetts House of Representatives, to which he was sent to oppose the division of Worcester County. In 1876 he was elected to Congress, where he served five terms. He then returned to the practice of law, in which he has been engaged to the present time, being senior member of the firm of Rice, King and Rice, in Worcester. He is a Director of the City National Bank, Vice-President of the People's Savings Bank, and a member of the Worcester Board of Trade. He is also a member of the Overseers of Bowdoin College, of the Trustees of Clark University, of the Worcester Polytechnic Institute, and of Leicester Academy.

He was married November 21, 1855, to Cornelia A. Moen, of Stamford, Connecticut. They had two children. (1) William Whitney Rice, born May 31, 1858, died February 10, 1864. (2) Charles Moen Rice, born in Worcester, November 6, 1860. He fitted for college at Exeter Academy, and graduated at Harvard University in 1882. He studied law at Harvard Law School, and in his father's office. He was admitted to the bar in Worcester in

February, 1886, and is now the junior member of the firm of Rice, King and Rice.

Cornelia A. Moen Rice died at Worcester, June 16, 1862, aged twenty-nine years and eight months.

Mr. Rice married for his second wife Alice Miller, daughter of Henry W. Miller, of Worcester, September 28, 1875. She was born in Worcester, July 22, 1840. They have had no children.

Mr. and Mrs. Rice spend a portion of the summer months on the old place in Winchendon, owned by Phinehas Whitney in 1802.

Lucy Ann Rice was married to Rev. Milan Hubbard Hitchcock, September 24, 1857. They have been missionaries at Ceylon and at Constantinople. They returned, that Mrs. Hitchcock might care for her mother in her extreme old age. They reside at Hubbardston, Mass. They have had no children.

Charles Jenkins Rice was married to Sarah M. Cummings, February 1, 1872. She was born in Winchendon, June 5, 1842. Mr. Rice always resided in Winchendon, on the place owned by his mother, which was a part of the old tavern property owned by Phinehas Whitney in 1802. He was engaged in the business of manufacturing and dealing in lumber. When a college education was offered him by his mother, he declined it, preferring to be a business man.

He was possessed of a great many of the traits of his grandfather, Phinehas Whitney. Old men used

to say, when they saw him walking across Winchendon common, that he reminded them of Capt.
Phinehas. He had the same instinctive knowledge
of land, of cattle and of horses, which seems to have
characterized his ancestors. His judgment of all
values was most correct and reliable, hence he was
frequently selected as appraiser of estates.

Independent in his own principles, he soon became a leading man in the town, and for many years
before his death was the regularly chosen moderator
of all the town meetings. Probably no man in town
had a greater influence than Mr. Rice.

He was a leading man in the church to which his
grandfather belonged, and was, like him, always the
friend and helper of the sick and needy.

He was an unswerving republican, and Winchendon always gave a very large majority to the
republican candidates during his life.

In 1884 he was elected to the Massachusetts House
of Representatives, to which he was re-elected.

He died May 3, 1892. He was buried in the same
lot with his father and mother in the old Winchendon burying-ground. They had no children.

William Barrett Whitney, son of Capt. Phinehas,
lived in Winchendon during the earlier part of his
life and was engaged in farming. Later in life he
moved to Orange, where he was engaged in the
manufacture of lumber and of wooden ware.

He was married December 20, 1827, to Lois Stone

of Fitzwilliam, N. H. While he resided in Winchendon he was a prosperous man, carrying on a business similar to that of his father and grandfather. After moving to Orange he built up a very large and prosperous business, his unusual knowledge of the values of land, especially of woodland, being of much advantage to him. He was always ready to buy land and to enter upon new business operations, with some of which he was unacquainted. Many of these were successful, but some of them were not, which resulted in his pecuniary embarrassment and the liquidation of his affairs, in which he was succeeded by his nephew and namesake, William Barrett Washburn, who continued with great success the business enterprise commenced by his uncle.

He was a man of kind nature, of great industry and ambitious to carry on a large business. After his embarrassment at Orange he sought new fields of enterprise in Warren, Penn., and ultimately in Vineland, N. J.

After the marriage of his daughters and the death of his wife he came back to his old home in Winchendon, where he spent some time with his nephew, Charles J. Rice, busying himself about the scenes of his childhood. He died at the house of his daughter, Elizabeth Ellen Stevens, in Cambridge, Massachusetts, February 15, 1874. He and his wife and their only son are buried in the Whitney corner of the old burying-ground.

They had four children, one son and three daughters, all born in Winchendon.

(1) Charles Milton Whitney was born December 31, 1828. He died at Orange, January 24, 1843.

(2) Elizabeth Ellen Whitney was born September 2, 1831. She died in infancy.

(3) Elizabeth Ellen Whitney, 2nd, was born August 2, 1834.

(4) Louisa Lyman Whitney was born August 8, 1836.

Elizabeth Ellen Whitney, 2nd, was married April 27, 1854, to Abraham W. Stevens, a Unitarian clergyman. He is now pursuing a literary life, residing at Cambridge. They have had three children, all boys.

(1) Harold W. Stevens, born January 26, 1859. He graduated at the Massachusetts Institute of Technology and is now engaged in the National Bank of the Republic, in Boston, Mass. He was married December 4, 1880, to Frances Elizabeth Ball. They have one child, Harold Parker Stevens, born in Cambridge, January 2, 1882.

(2) Charles Herbert Stevens, born in Barre, April 20, 1860. He graduated at Harvard College in 1882. He is engaged in the Law Publishing House of C. C. Soule in Boston.

(3) Ralph Leslie Stevens, born in Cambridge, November 10, 1870, is still pursuing his studies.

Louisa Lyman Whitney, youngest daughter of William Barrett Whitney, was married September 4, 1855, to Jason Asbury Morrison. He died May 15, 1865.

They had but one child, a son named William Barrett Morrison, born in Warren, Penn., April 8, 1863. Being of delicate health his mother removed with him to Denver, Col., where he has since been engaged in the State National Bank.

Mary Whitney, third daughter of Capt. Phinehas and Bethiah Whitney, was married at Winchendon, January 22, 1828, to Alvah Godding, M. D. She died in Winchendon, November 15, 1870.

They moved in early life from the old centre to the new village, where she was the leader in society and in all good works and charities. In her youth she was called handsome on account of her vivacity and quickness of motion. She always took a great interest in public affairs, and I doubt if any man in Winchendon was better posted in them than she. Always hospitable and generous, her home was a favorite resort for many friends.

Dr. Godding, her husband, was a physician of the old school. He rode a large circuit, upon which I do not think there was a better loved man than himself. He ministered to the sick, not only to their diseases but also to their necessities, and his carriage carried to the houses of his patients baskets of food and dainties from his own house as often as pills and purgatives from the apothecaries. He died in Winchendon January 11, 1875.

They had one son, William Whitney Godding, born in Winchendon, May 5, 1831. He graduated at Dartmouth College in 1854. He completed his studies at Castleton Medical College, Vermont, where he graduated in 1857. He practiced his profession for some years in Winchendon and in Fitchburg, but he early became attracted to practice for the insane. He was assistant physician at the New Hampshire Asylum for the Insane at Concord from 1859 to 1862. In 1863 he was appointed assistant physician at the Government Hospital for the Insane at Washington known as St. Elizabeth's. In 1870 he was appointed Superintendent of the State Lunatic Asylum at Taunton, Massachusetts, where he remained seven years. In 1877 he was recalled to Washington where he was appointed Superintendent of the Government Hospital for the Insane, which position he still holds. There are few posts of greater care and responsibility than that occupied by Dr. Godding, and he is at the present time recognized as one of the first authorities in the country on the subject of insanity.

He married on December 4, 1860, Ellen Roanah Murdock of Winchendon. They have had three children, two daughters and one son.

(1) Mary Patten Godding, born February 22, 1867.

(2) Rowena Murdock Godding, born July 7, 1870.

(3) Alvah Godding, born February 8, 1872.

They reside in Washington, although Dr. Godding always intends to spend a portion of the summer in his native town.

Sarah Ann Whitney, the fourth daughter of Capt. Phinehas and Bethiah Whitney, was first married, August 28, 1832, to Josiah Brown of Winchendon. He was a man very much respected by his townsmen. He died September 29, 1836. They had one son who died in infancy.

She married for her second husband, April 23, 1839, Capt. Charles W. Bigelow, of Winchendon. They had one son, Charles Edwin Bigelow, born March 18, 1843.

He graduated at Williams College in 1866. He was married to Jennie Mary Robbins of Groton, June 23, 1868. They had one child who died on the day he was born. They reside in New York City, spending their summers in the beautiful town of Groton.

He is President of the Knowles Steam Pump Works in New York, where he has been since 1867. He is a very able and energetic business man, and occupies positions of financial trust in New York City.

Louisa Whitney, the youngest daughter of Capt. Phinehas and Bethiah Whitney, was married

December 4, 1835, to Rev. Giles Lyman, a Congregational clergyman. They had no children. He died in Winchendon November 16, 1872. She died December 5, 1892, at the house of her nephew, Charles J. Rice, on the spot where she was born.

Here I end the record of the descendants of Phinehas and Bethiah Whitney. I recollect them all. I consider my grandfather and grandmother as very remarkable persons, and as I review their descendants I do not think they have proved unworthy of their origin. The five daughters of Capt. Phinehas and Bethiah each filled notable places in society, and each of them filled those places worthily.

They are all gone now and they will soon be forgotten, but their children and grandchildren who knew them will never forget them.

After investigating the history of a family we become interested in the family traits as far as we have observed them, and I feel an interest in the Whitney family on account of the hasty and imperfect investigations which have resulted in these records, and because I am one of the family.

I imagine that there is always a certain type which belongs to a family which may be traced in the different ramifications of the family, of course modified very much by the associations and connections, but still retaining through all something of a permanent individuality. Some families are of stronger character, more marked peculiarities than others, and I am pleased to imagine that this peculiarity lasts in the race through many generations. Especially do I find an enduring strength in the old English families. They were a strong type of men who came here. It required self-reliance, boldness, determination, to abandon the country of their birth, where their fathers had dwelt, and cross the ocean to settle in a new and untried country, and those characteristics were increased by the peculiar experiences through which they were called upon to pass in their new home.

I do not think that the Whitney family was remarkable above other families for prominence in these characteristics, but it seems to me that I can see evidences wherever I find them of certain uniform traits which, to me, go to make up a Whitney individuality. Heredity is one of the most remarkable elements of humanity, and I fancy that some characteristics which existed in the family in old England have continued to exist in New England.

I mention among these, first, that the family has increased and greatly multiplied in numbers. This is a remark applicable also to all families which we can trace with any degree of continuity. I find that there are very many Whitneys throughout England, and also through all the countries settled by English speaking men. It is said that thirty-two thousand descendants of old John Whitney of

Watertown may be found in the United States, and how many uncounted thousands have been in the home country and other countries of the English people!

I think that the Whitneys are, physically, a strong race. This does not mean, of course, that there are not and have not been a great many weak and unhealthy members of the race, but I think that old Torstinus, founder of the family, has not entirely passed away from among his descendants. As we have seen, he was a hardy Norman, warlike, trusted by his King, and as long as I can trace the line of those who directly inherited his manor and his property, they seem to have belonged to the type of their ancestor. Of course, as I have said, a family type is modified by location, by intermarriages, and by the thousand circumstances which attend the lives of all, but wherever I find Whitneys I find that their prevailing physical characteristic is strength and endurance.

Second, I think that in the various communities where they have lived they have maintained a respectable position, never attaining any very marked prominence, but still assuming and faithfully performing the duties of respectable and efficient members of the societies where they have lived.

Again, I think that they have generally shown a capacity for affairs rather more than ordinary among their associates. I think they have possessed ten-

dencies to engage in agricultural employments.
Wherever I find them I find them with good farms
and especially good farm buildings. Very often,
rather oftener I think than with most families, they
built in the town where they found early settlement,
large houses, generally square-built farmhouses,
which seemed to satisfy them without much addition
of exterior ornament.

Old John Whitney of Watertown acquired large
landed property, much of which was distributed
among his children during life, and this characteristic to acquire land and cattle seems to have been a
leading one with the family.

The family seems to have evinced rather remarkable mechanical skill. Eli Whitney has been said to
have produced a greater change in affairs than almost any other man. His invention of the cotton-
gin made cotton a king. Upon the vast increase of
the cotton crop in the South, caused by his invention,
the system of slavery sprang into a mighty power
and maintained itself against all the influences of
civilization for generations. In after life he still
evinced the same mechanical ingenuity, the products
of which may still be seen in the village which he
established in Connecticut and the manufacturing
establishments there which have grown out of his
enterprise. I note many other Whitneys whose mechanical skill has been of national importance.

Quite early in the history of the country the

Whitneys were marked by the desire of obtaining liberal education, and I think that we should find in the list of college graduates quite as great a number of this name as of almost any other.

They have held high places in the church and in the mercantile life of the cities. In New York and Boston the Whitney family has furnished many of the most enterprising and respectable merchants.

I would sum up all by saying that the family has, from the beginning, maintained itself among the first in position among its neighbors, in enterprise in the various kinds of business into which it has entered, and in maintaining a constant character of usefulness and successful enterprise in the various communities where its members have been found.

I think that the old Norman from whom the family sprang was a sturdy, well-developed warrior, of fully average size and strength, with light hair and light complexion, and that this type of physique has come down from him to the present generation in a marked degree.

While there is nothing to be proud of, nothing to excite a boastful feeling among the American Whitneys, I would say that they have all maintained themselves in such a manner that no one need blush that he is obliged to recognize his relations to that family rather than to others that have had higher positions in wealth and worldly honor.